Pippa's Day At The Beach With **Percy** The Pelican

Written by: Jennifer Lynn Goel

Illustrated by: Andriana Polukhina

Pippa's Day At The Beach With **Percy** The Pelican

Written by: Jennifer Lynn Goel
Illustrated by: Andriana Polukhina

ISBN: 979-8474485478

DEDICATION

This book is dedicated to my children,
Krishna, Anya and Maya.
I love you until the end of the universe.

Jennifer Lynn Goel

Pippa's day started off like most summer days, a fun filled day full of adventure at the beach.

Pippa and her mom had set out for the beach. On their walk they discovered so many neat things. Pippa first noticed all the tall grass growing along the boardwalk.

As they continued to walk along the boardwalk, Pippa smiled and with so much excitement in her voice and yelled "Look mom, the beach!"

Pippa ran as fast as she could to the end of the boardwalk and pushed her little toes deep into the warm sand.

Pippa grabbed her mom's hand and couldn't contain her excitement as the next big surprise she saw was big beautiful waves crashing into the shore.

Along the shore Pippa discovered so many amazing things in the sand. She found a dollar bill, seaweed, sticks and even saw a few crabs walking around.

Pippa sat down in the warm sand, took her shovel and pail and began to dig looking for more treasures.

Pippa was digging and digging and digging when all of the sudden she yelled "Look mom, so many shells!"

Pippa was enjoying her day at the beach when she heard a noise off in the distance. Pippa took her shovel and pail and began to walk towards the noise in the distance.

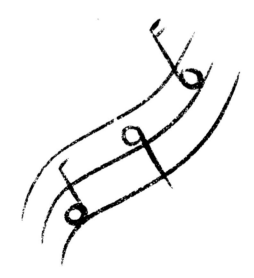

Pippa and her mom walked a little farther and off in the distance they saw something laying in the sand.

As Pippa and her mom got closer they could see it was a big beautiful pelican who was stuck in a net. Pippa and her mom ran over to the pelican and began to think about how they could help untangle it.

Pippa could see the pelican was sad and scared. She began to sing hoping to calm it down.

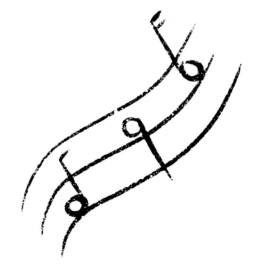

Pippa had soothed the pelican enough that her mom was able to remove the net it was trapped in.

As Pippa and her mom began slowly backing away, they heard a faint voice come from the pelican. They both looked at each other and smiled. "Thank you," the pelican said.

Pippa's eyes grew as big as the sun, "You can talk?" she said, "Yes" the pelican replied, "My name is Percy, Percy the pelican and I want to thank you for helping me, now I can fly home to see my family."

Pippa looked at her mom with disbelief and said to Percy, "Today was my day at the beach with my mom, we were going on an adventure and heard a noise, it was you, you needed our help."

"Where is your home?" she asked Percy. "My home is this beach, my family and I all live here, but we have to be careful as sometimes humans leave trash and it can hurt us."

Pippa looked at her mom with sadness in her eyes and said to Percy, "I am sorry us humans do not take good care of our beaches, I am just happy we were able to help you so you can return home to your family."

Off in the distance Pippa and
her mom could see the trash that
littered the beautiful beach.

Pippa took her mom's hand, looked at her mom and said "I had a great day at the beach mom, I'm so happy we were able to save Percy the pelican."

Pippa and her mom walked towards the boardwalk, shovel and pail in hand and headed home.

THE END

Made in the USA
Middletown, DE
30 October 2021